Katie and the Class Pet

by Fran Manushkin

illustrated by Tammie Lyon

PICTURE WINDOW BOOKS
a capstone imprint

Katie Woo is published by Picture Window Books,
1710 Roe Crest Drive
North Mankato, Minnesota 56003
www.capstonepub.com

Text © 2012 Fran Manushkin
Illustrations © 2012 Picture Window Books

Library of Congress Cataloging-in-Publication Data
Manushkin, Fran.
 Katie and the class pet / by Fran Manushkin; illustrated by Tammie Lyon.
     p. cm. — (Katie Woo)
 Summary: When Katie is chosen to take the class pet, Binky the guinea pig, home for the weekend, she runs into a problem.
ISBN 978-1-4048-6520-4 (library binding)
ISBN 978-1-4048-6856-4 (pbk.)
 [1. Guinea pigs—Fiction. 2. Schools—Fiction. 3. Chinese Americans—Fiction.] I. Lyon, Tammie, ill. II. Title.
 PZ7.M3195Kah 2011
 [E]—dc22   2011005487

Art Director: Kay Fraser
Graphic Designer: Emily Harris

Printed in the United States of America in Stevens Point, Wisconsin.
052012
006770R

Table of Contents

Chapter 1

The Perfect Pet

One day, Miss Winkle

asked, "Who would like to

have a class pet?"

"I would!" yelled everyone.

"I want a pony," said

Katie. "We could ride him at

recess!"

"A pony is too big," said Miss Winkle. "We need a pet that fits in our room."

"How about a rabbit?" asked JoJo.

"Or a mouse," said Pedro.

"I'll think about it," said Miss Winkle.

A few days later, Miss
Winkle came in with a cage.

"Our class pet is inside,"
she said. "Can you guess
what it is?"

"A bunch of ants?" asked
Pedro.

"A skunk?" joked Barry.

"Surprise!" said Miss

Winkle. "It's a guinea pig."

"He's so cute," said JoJo.

"Let's name him Binky,"

said Katie. "The name is cute

and little, like him."

"Binky! Binky! Binky!"

everyone shouted.

"Binky it is!" said Miss

Winkle.

Chapter 2
Katie Takes Binky Home

Binky let everyone hold

him. He made happy,

squeaky noises.

He liked going to school.

He loved music time best. He

always squeaked along.

Every Friday, Miss Winkle

took Binky home for the

weekend. But one Friday, she

said, "I'm going away this

weekend. I need someone to

take Binky home."

"Me! Me! Me!"

yelled everyone.

Miss Winkle pulled a

name from a hat. Katie Woo

won!

"Binky, I'll take good care

of you," she promised.

Katie put Binky's cage in
her room. She fed him guinea-
pig pellets and grapes and
cucumbers.

Then she and Binky played
games.

"Keep the doors and windows closed," said Katie's dad. "We don't want Binky to get lost."

That night, Katie fell

asleep in her bed, and Binky

slept in his house.

Katie played with Binky

all weekend.

On Sunday, she said,

"Binky, I'd love to keep you,

but you belong to our class.

They would miss you."

Chapter 3

A Lost Guinea Pig

On Monday morning,

Katie took Binky out of his

cage one last time.

"Uh-oh," she said. "I have

to go to the bathroom."

When Katie came back,

Binky was gone! Katie

looked under the bed and

everywhere. No Binky!

The window was open

a crack. "He must have

escaped!" Katie cried.

Katie felt terrible. "What will I tell my class?" she said. "I promised to take good care of Binky."

Katie picked up her backpack and headed out the door.

Katie walked to her classroom slowly. "I hope I never get there," she said.

But she did.

Miss Winkle asked, "Katie, how was your weekend with Binky?"

"Um, I have some bad news . . ." Katie began.

Then she started to cry.

Suddenly, Katie
felt something
on her neck. It
was warm and
soft. It was Binky,
poking out of her backpack!

"So that's where you
went!" Katie smiled. "You
were getting ready to come
to school!"

"Katie," asked Miss Winkle, "what's the bad news you were going to tell us?"

"It's not bad anymore!" Katie laughed. "It's funny!"

And she told them the whole happy story.

About the Author

Fran Manushkin is the author of many
popular picture books, including *How Mama
Brought the Spring; Baby, Come Out!; Latkes
and Applesauce: A Hanukkah Story;* and *The
Tushy Book.* There is a real Katie Woo — she's
Fran's great-niece — but she never gets in
half the trouble of the Katie Woo in the books.
Fran writes on her beloved Mac computer in New York City,
without the help of her two naughty cats, Miss Chippie
and Goldy.

About the Illustrator

Tammie Lyon began her love for drawing
at a young age while sitting at the
kitchen table with her dad. She continued
her love of art and eventually attended
the Columbus College of Art and Design,
where she earned a bachelors degree in fine
art. After a brief career as a professional
ballet dancer, she decided to devote herself full time to
illustration. Today she lives with her husband, Lee, in Cincinnati,
Ohio. Her dogs, Gus and Dudley, keep her company as she works
in her studio.

Glossary

cucumbers (KYOO-kuhm-burz)—long, green vegetables with soft centers filled with seeds

guinea pig (GIN-ee PIG)—a small mammal with smooth fur, short ears, and a very short tail, often kept as a pet

recess (REE-sess)—a break from work for rest and relaxation

squeaky (SKWEE-kee)—high-pitched or shrill sounding

terrible (TER-uh-buhl)—very bad or unpleasant

Discussion Questions

1. Do you think a guinea pig was a good choice for a class pet? Why or why not?

2. What sort of pet would you like to have?

3. If one of your classmates lost the class pet or something else that was important to your class, what would you do? What would you say?

Writing Prompts

1. Do you think Binky is a good name for a guinea pig? Make a list of five other names. Then circle your favorite.

2. Make a "Lost Pet" poster for Binky. Be sure to include a picture of him and a description.

3. Imagine Miss Winkle brought the class a pet skunk, like Barry joked. What would happen next? Write a story about it.

A Guinea Pig of Your Own!

With this fun project you can make your own guinea pig out of an old sock and some dryer lint! Sounds crazy, right? But your pet will be *so* cute. I promise!

What you need:

- an old, short sock
- stuffing, like cotton balls or fiberfill
- a needle
- thread
- craft glue
- dryer lint (Ask a grown-up where to find this soft, fuzzy stuff. It comes out of your clothes dryer!)
- googly eyes
- dark marker

What you do:

1. Fill your sock with stuffing. This will be your guinea pig's body, so make it as fat as you would like.

2. Tuck the top of the sock in, and then ask a grown-up to sew the hole shut with a needle and thread.

3. Working in small sections, apply some craft glue to the sock. Then cover the glue with dryer lint. Repeat until the whole sock is covered. Let dry.

4. To finish your project, glue googly eyes on your pet. With the marker, draw a nose on your pet.

You can even make your guinea pig a little bed lined with shredded paper, grass, or hay. Be sure to give your pet lots of love, but don't worry about feeding it!

THE FUN DOESN'T STOP HERE!

Discover more at www.capstonekids.com

💜 Videos & Contests

✿ Games & Puzzles

💜 Friends & Favorites

✿ Authors & Illustrators

Find cool websites and more books like this one at www.facthound.com. Just type in the Book ID: 9781404865204 and you're ready to go!